Let's go to the Swings

Level 2E

Written by Lucy George
Illustrated by Andrew Geeson

Ticktock

What is synthetic phonics?

Synthetic phonics teaches children to recognise the sounds of letters and to blend (synthesise) them together to make whole words.

Understanding sound/letter relationships gives children the confidence and ability to read unfamiliar words, without having to rely on memory or guesswork; this helps them progress towards independent reading.

Did you know? Spoken English uses more than 40 speech sounds. Each sound is called a *phoneme*. Some phonemes relate to a single letter (d-o-g) and others to combinations of letters (sh-ar-p). When a phoneme is written down it is called a *grapheme*. Teaching these sounds, matching them to their written form and sounding out words for reading is the basis of synthetic phonics.

Consultant

I love reading phonics has been created in consultation with language expert Abigail Steel. She has a background in teaching and teacher training and is a respected expert in the field of Synthetic Phonics. Abigail Steel is a regular contributor to educational publications. Her international education consultancy supports parents and teachers in the promotion of literacy skills.

Reading tips

This book focuses on the ng sound as in ring.

Tricky words in this book

Any words in bold may have unusual spellings or are new and have not yet been introduced.

Tricky words in this book:

go to the be they play park bees she where were

Extra ways to have fun with this book

After the reader has finished the story, ask them questions about what they have just read:

What was the name of the puppy in the story?
What did Anna and Kit play on in the park?

Explain that the two letters 'ng' make one sound. Think of other words that use the 'ng' sound, such as *sting* and *sing*.

I like creeping through long, tall grass. Sometimes I think I am a tiger!

A pronunciation guide

This grid highlights the sounds used in the story and offers a guide on how to say them.

s as in sat	a as in ant	t as in tin	p as in pig	i as in ink
n as in net	c as in cat	e as in egg	h as in hen	r as in rat
m as in mug	d as in dog	g as in get	o as in ox	u as in up
l as in log	f as in fan	b as in bag	j as in jug	v as in van
w as in wet	z as in zip	y as in yet	k as in kit	qu as in quick
x as in box	ff as in off	ll as in ball	ss as in kiss	zz as in buzz
ck as in duck	pp as in puppy	nn as in bunny	rr as in arrow	gg as in egg
dd as in daddy	bb as in chubby	tt as in attic	sh as in shop	ch as in chip
th as in them	th as in thin	ng as in sing		

Be careful not to add an 'uh' sound to 's', 't', 'p', 'c', 'h', 'r', 'm', 'd', 'g', 'l', 'f' and 'b'. For example, say 'fff' not 'fuh' and 'sss' not 'suh'.

Anna and Kit **go to the** swings.

Kit can not **be** long.

Anna tells Kit to run. “Hurry!”

Anna is bossy!

Kit brings her dog Jim. Jim is
a puppy.

They get to the swings and Jim zips off among the swings.

Anna and Kit **play** on all the things in the **park**.

Jim runs at a fox. The fox is very quick.

Anna and Kit hang.

Jim runs at the **bees**.

The bees buzz.

Anna and Kit cling.

Jim runs at a kitten.

The kitten is chubby.

Anna and Kit swing on the swings and sing a song.

“The big swing is the best!”

Kit swings up and up.

“I am the king!” **she** sings.

But **where** is Jim?

Jim runs at a buggy! Kit yells
at Jim to stop.

Anna and Kit run back. Jim runs along. The swings **were** fun!

OVER 48 TITLES IN SIX LEVELS
Abigail Steel recommends...

Some titles from Level 1

978-1-84898-600-8

978-1-84898-603-9

978-1-78325-098-1

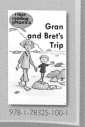

978-1-78325-100-1

Other titles to enjoy from Level 2

978-1-84898-605-3

978-1-84898-607-7

978-1-78325-101-8

Some titles from Level 3

978-1-78325-105-6

978-1-84898-609-1

978-1-84898-610-7

978-1-78325-108-7

An Hachette UK Company
www.hachette.co.uk

First published in Great Britain in 2012 by TickTock, an imprint of Octopus Publishing Group Ltd,
Endeavour House, 189 Shaftesbury Avenue, London WC2H 8JY.
www.octopusbooks.co.uk
www.ticktockbooks.co.uk

ISBN 978 1 78325 102 5

Printed and bound in China
10 9 8 7 6 5 4 3